NINTENDO ®
HEROES

Mario and the Incredible Rescue

NINTENDO HEROES

Mario and the Incredible Rescue

By Tracey West

SCHOLASTIC INC.

New York   Toronto   London   Auckland   Sydney
Mexico City   New Delhi   Hong Kong   Buenos Aires

No part of this publication may be reproduced in whole or in part, stored in a
retrieval system, or transmitted in any form or by any means, electronic, mechanical,
photocopying, recording, or otherwise, without written permission of the publisher.
For information regarding permission, write to Scholastic Inc., Attention: Permissions
Department, 557 Broadway, New York, NY 10012.

ISBN 0-439-84366-9

Published by Scholastic Inc.
SCHOLASTIC and associated logos are trademarks and/or
registered trademarks of Scholastic Inc.

12 11 10 9 8 7 6   8 9 10/0

Printed in the U.S.A.
First printing, May 2006

Princess Peach Needs Help!

"Ah, what a beautiful morning," Mario said as he stepped out of his house. Before him, the Mushroom Kingdom sparkled in the morning sunlight. The sky above was almost as blue as Mario's overalls.

Mario's brother, Luigi, walked up next to him. With his brown mustache and round nose, Luigi looked like a taller, thinner version of Mario.

"What do you want to do today, Mario?" Luigi asked.

Mario took a deep breath of fresh air. "Nothing," he said. "Absolutely nothing. The

Mushroom Kingdom is safe. Nobody is causing any trouble. Princess Peach is safe in her castle. For once, you and I can just relax, okay?"

Luigi frowned. "I don't know about that, Mario," he said. "Look!"

A tiny figure was running toward them, zigzagging up the pathway. He wore white shorts and a blue vest. A round, sweet face peeked out from under a big cap that looked like a red polka-dotted mushroom.

"It's Toad!" Mario cried, easily spotting their good friend. "What does he want? He's in a big hurry!"

"Mario! Luigi! I'm so glad I found you!" Toad said. He took a breath after every word. "Princess Peach needs your help!"

"Oh no!" Luigi cried.

"Calm down, Toad," Mario said. "Tell us what happened."

"I saw it with my own eyes!" Toad began, waving his tiny arms. "Princess Peach was walking in her garden. Her guards were all

around her. But then these things came up . . . ," Toad looked like he might faint.

"What kind of *things*?" Mario asked.

"G-g-g-ghosts!" Toad said, shivering. "They had spooky eyes. They floated in the air. I could s-s-see right through them!"

Luigi turned pale. "Are you sure they were ghosts?"

Toad nodded. "They had to be! The princess's guards tried to fight them, but they couldn't even touch them! The ghosts grabbed Princess Peach. Then they flew away."

"Where did they take her?" Luigi asked.

Mario looked grim. "I bet I know," he said. "Bowser's got something to do with this, right?"

"Yes, they flew right toward Bowser's Keep," Toad replied.

Mario shook his fist. "That big bully!" he said. "I'll teach him to leave Princess Peach alone once and for all."

Luigi looked worried. "Are you sure we can do it, Mario?" he asked.

"No problem," Mario said. "We've saved Princess Peach from Bowser before."

"I d-d-d-don't know, Mario," Toad said. "Those ghosts were so scary! I've never seen anything like them before. Even the princess's guards couldn't fight them! How are we supposed to defeat them?"

"We'll find a way," Mario said. He sighed. "So much for doing nothing today. Let's go save Princess Peach!"

Mario marched down the path. Luigi and Toad hesitated. They looked at each other. They were both thinking the same thing: *ghosts?*

"We've got to help the princess," Luigi said finally.

"I know," said Toad.

Then they headed down the path after Mario.

The Sorceress

Mario stopped in front of a big metal pipe. "Let's take a shortcut," he said. "This pipe should lead us right to the Kero Sewers. And then we won't be too far from Bowser's Keep."

"Isn't it dark down there, Mario?" Luigi asked. "What if the ghosts are hiding down there?"

"Then we'll show them what we're made of," Mario said. He hopped into the pipe. "Let's go!"

Mario slid down the pipe, his feet thudding as they hit bottom. Luigi was right — it *was* dark down there. As Mario waited for his eyes

to adjust to the darkness, he heard Luigi and Toad thump behind him.

Mario had taken this path before. It was a good shortcut, and he was a plumber, after all. He felt comfortable around pipes. This one led to an underground passageway made out of bricks. The brick path stretched out before them; there was nowhere to go but straight ahead.

Mario walked quickly down the path. There was no time to waste. He didn't like the idea of Princess Peach being in Bowser's clutches — especially if what Toad said was true, and there were ghosts involved. Princess Peach was as sweet as the fruit she was named for. Under her rule, the Mushroom Kingdom was a happy place. If Bowser tried to hurt her —

"Mario! Luigi! Stop!" Toad cried. "I hear something."

Mario slowed down. "Toad, I don't think there are any ghosts in this tunnel."

But then a shuffling sound reached his

ears. There was something up ahead — but Mario didn't think it was the ghosts.

The shuffling sound came closer. Mario sighed. "I should have known," he said.

Three tiny creatures came toward them in the dark. They looked like brown mushrooms with black shoes and angry eyes.

"Little Goombas!" Mario said. "Can't you see we're in a hurry?"

Luigi knew just what to do, too. "Toad, hop on my back," he said. Quickly, Toad obeyed.

"Sorry, Little Goombas," Mario said. He jumped up and stomped on the first one. He jumped again and stomped on the second one. Behind him, Luigi stomped on the third Little Goomba.

Mario glanced back at the stunned Little Goombas. "That was easy," he said.

"Maybe, Mario," Luigi said. "But it looks like things are about to get harder!"

The friends had come to a T in the tunnel. They could go either left or right. Luigi

pointed to the left tunnel as a small army of Little Goombas raced toward them!

"Run!" Mario yelled. Stomping on three Little Goombas was no problem, but defeating a whole army of them wouldn't be so easy. Mario zipped into the tunnel on the right, and Luigi followed, with Toad still on his back.

Mario ran as far and fast as he could — and then came to a screeching halt. The tunnel was blocked by a brick wall.

"What do we do now, Mario?" Luigi asked.

"We kick!" Mario shouted. He jumped, spun around, and started kicking the wall in front of him. Toad jumped off of Luigi's back and kicked the wall on the right.

When the friends broke through, they found a small chamber with a glittering gold coin inside.

"Nice!" said Luigi. He grabbed the coin and stuffed it into a pocket.

Mario grunted and started to break the next wall. The coin was a good find, but it wouldn't help them fight off the Little Goombas. He

could hear the sound of their tiny feet running closer and closer.

Mario, Luigi, and Toad managed to open up a small hole in the next wall. Mario peered through and found himself looking at a dark forest. It didn't look familiar — but they didn't have a choice.

"Let's go!" Mario called. He picked up Toad and pushed him through the hole. Then he and Luigi crawled through it.

"We've got to block up the hole, or the Little Goombas will come after us!" Mario warned.

But when he turned around, the brick wall was no longer there.

Mario blinked. They had just crawled through a brick tunnel, right? But there was no sign of the tunnel or the wall anywhere. Tall trees rose up around them in every direction. The trees blocked most of the sunlight above them, which made the forest look gloomy and dark. Mario shivered, although he wasn't sure why.

He turned back to Luigi and Toad, who appeared to be just as puzzled as he was.

"That's strange," Mario said finally.

"I don't like this at all," Toad said. "Do we even know where we are?"

Luigi pointed into the trees. "I'm not sure," he said. "But I see a light in there."

Mario thought for a moment. He had never been in these woods before. He didn't know where to go — but they had to go *somewhere*. Following the light was their only chance. "Let's see what's there," Mario suggested.

The forest was eerily quiet as they walked through the trees. Soon they saw that the light was coming from a small stone cottage. Mario walked up to the door and raised his fist to knock.

"What if there are g-g-ghosts in there?" Toad asked.

Mario sighed. "Then maybe they can give us directions."

He knocked on the door.

"Come in!" a woman's voice called from inside.

"That doesn't sound like a ghost," Luigi said cautiously.

"There's only one way to find out," Mario said. He pushed open the door.

They stepped inside and saw a hooded figure sitting at a table. On the table, a single candle flickered, casting shadows on the figure's dark robe.

"Sit down," the figure said. "I know what you are doing. And I can help you."

"You do?" Toad asked. Mario sat down first. He could see the wrinkled face of an old woman under the hood. Luigi and Toad didn't want to sit, but Mario motioned for them to join him.

"I can help you defeat the ghosts and save Princess Peach," said the old woman. "But my help will cost you."

"But we have nothing for you," Mario said. "Unless you maybe need some help with your plumbing."

But Luigi reached into his pocket and pulled out the gold coin he had found in the tunnel. "How about this?" he asked.

"That will do," the woman replied. She reached out a bony hand and took the coin from Luigi. She placed the coin inside her robes, then took down her hood to reveal two glittering green eyes.

"I am Cybele the Sorceress," she said. "Not long ago, Bowser stumbled across my forest. He stole a book from me — *The Book of Spells*. He used it to conjure up an army of ghosts."

"I knew they were ghosts!" Toad cried.

"If they are ghosts, then how can we fight them?" Mario asked.

"There is only one way to defeat them," Cybele replied. She spread out a piece of brown parchment on the table. The parchment showed a drawing of six mushrooms, with words written beneath them.

"The ghosts can be defeated with a spell," Cybele continued. "To perform the spell, you

must gather six mushrooms from different locations in the Mushroom Kingdom. With the six mushrooms in hand, recite the words of the spell. The ghosts will be cast back into their realm."

Luigi lifted his cap and scratched his head. "How are we supposed to find the six mushrooms?"

"You will find clues," Cybele said. She handed Mario a piece of flat wood shaped like a mushroom. "This is your first clue. It will lead you to the first mushroom."

Then Cybele gave Mario a blue pouch with long straps. "Use this to carry the mushrooms," she said.

"I don't know," Mario said. "This all sounds very strange. Mushrooms? Spells? How do we know you are telling the truth?"

Cybele's green eyes narrowed. "Watch," she said.

The sorceress reached out toward the candle in the middle of the table. Her thin fingers

waved at the candle. The candlelight swirled and grew brighter. Suddenly, an image appeared in the flames.

It was Bowser! A metal cage hung from the ceiling above him, with Princess Peach trapped inside! Six ghosts guarded her.

"The princess!" Toad cried.

The sorceress waved her fingers, and the image disappeared.

"I do not lie," she said. "Find the mushrooms. And hurry, before it is too late."

"Thank you, ma'am," Luigi said. He and Toad stood up. Mario started to follow them, but Cybele grabbed his arm.

"I have one more thing for you," she said. She placed a white envelope in his hand. "Your task will not be easy," she said. "Open this — but only if there is no hope left."

Mario stared at the envelope for a second before putting it in his pouch. He slung the pouch over his shoulders.

"Thank you," Mario said. Then he turned

and left the cabin. He was glad that they had found a way to save the princess — but the sorceress's words haunted him.

If there is no hope left.

What did she mean?

The Kero Sewers

Luigi and Toad gathered around Mario. "What does the clue say?" Toad asked.

Mario looked at the clue carved into the flat piece of wood:

S R E W E S   O R E K
Go backward for the answer.

Mario studied the clue for a moment. Then he smiled. "That's easy! The clue is Kero Sewers spelled backward! We were going there anyway."

"But we're lost, remember?" Luigi said.

Mario frowned. "That's right." He didn't know how to find the sewers now.

Then Toad hopped up and down. "Look! Over there!"

Toad pointed through the trees, where a large sewer pipe rose out of the ground. Mario was sure it hadn't been there before.

"Let's go!" Mario called. He ran to the pipe and jumped in. Luigi and Toad jumped in after him.

Now they found themselves inside the Kero Sewers, a complicated maze of tunnels. Pipes jutted out from the floor, the walls, and even the ceiling.

"How are we supposed to find a mushroom in here?" Luigi asked.

"We walk, and we look," Mario said.

The friends slowly walked through the sewers. Mario walked past a pipe when a plant poked its head out. Startled, Mario jumped back.

The red plant had a large flower bulb on

top of a thick stem. The bulb was open like a wide mouth, and rows of sharp, pointed teeth lined each side!

"Where there are pipes, there are piranhas," Mario said. These plants loved to chomp on anything that got near them. He called back to Luigi and Toad. "Stay clear of the pipes!"

The friends walked on. Toad jumped skittishly every time a piranha plant stuck its head out of a pipe.

Mario started to wonder if the sorceress had been telling the truth. Finding a single mushroom inside the sewers would not be easy. Maybe she was working with Bowser, leading them on a wild goose chase. . . .

Then something dark and sparkly caught his eye: A black mushroom glittered in the distance. "That's it!" Mario cried. He ran toward the mushroom — and stopped just in time.

The path in front of him had ended. A deep ravine separated him from the mushroom.

There was only one way to cross the gap. Four large pipes jutted out from the bottom of the ravine. They could jump from pipe to pipe to get to the other side.

Luigi knew what he was thinking. "It won't be easy, Mario," he said. "Look!"

A red piranha plant poked its head out of the first pipe. As it ducked back under, another plant poked its head from the second pipe. A third plant poked out from the third pipe, and then a fourth plant rose from the fourth pipe. The plants moved in rhythm.

Mario sighed. He would have to time his jumps exactly right. If he didn't . . . GULP! He'd be piranha plant food.

"I'll go first," Mario said bravely. He watched the pipes carefully as the plants popped out. One, two, three, four. One, two, three, four. . . .

"One!" Mario cried, jumping. He landed on top of the pipe just as the piranha ducked inside.

"Two!" Mario jumped again, landing just

after the second plant disappeared from sight.

"Three!" He jumped and landed on the third pipe, but his footing wasn't as steady. He struggled to keep his balance. . . .

"Four!" Mario jumped on the fourth pipe just in time. Then he heaved himself onto the ledge on the other side of the ravine.

"You can do it, Luigi!" Mario called out.

Luigi nodded. Mario knew his brother was a good jumper. Luigi bent down, and Toad climbed on his back. Toad closed his eyes tightly.

Mario held his breath as Luigi and Toad jumped on the first pipe. Then the second pipe. Then the third pipe. . . .

The third pipe wobbled, just like it had done under Mario's feet. Toad began to slide off of Luigi's back. Luigi grabbed him.

"Mario, catch!"

Luigi tossed Toad over the fourth pipe. Mario held out his arms and caught him. The two slammed backward onto the ledge.

Luigi quickly jumped to the fourth plant, but his timing was off. The piranha plant began to open its mouth. Luigi lost his footing. He tried to jump to the ledge, but he fell short!

Mario dropped Toad and quickly thrust out his arm. "Hang on, Luigi!"

Luigi grabbed Mario's arm just in time. Mario hoisted him up to the ledge.

"Good job," Mario said. "Now it's time to get what we came for."

Mario reached down and plucked the glittering black mushroom.

A Song for Toadofski

As Mario lifted up the mushroom, a band of glittering light swirled underneath it. Another mushroom-shaped clue magically appeared in the middle of the light. Mario grabbed it with his free hand, and the light vanished.

Mario put the black mushroom in the pouch the sorceress had given him. Then he examined the clue.

"It says, 'Look in a place where Frogs and Toads live in harmony,'" Mario read. He began to think. "Frogs and Toads . . . harmony . . . I've got it!"

"What did you get?" Luigi asked with confusion.

"Frogfucius and Toadofski both live in Tadpole Pond. Toadofski composes beautiful music there — *harmony*, get it?" Mario answered.

"I get it," Luigi replied. "But how do we get there?"

Mario looked down the path ahead of them. "We need to go to the Midas River," he said. "I think it's this way."

They walked on, being careful to steer clear of any pipes they passed. Soon the sound of rushing water filled their ears. The path broke off to the right, and Mario took the turn, heading in the direction of the water.

Up ahead, he could see another ledge. Beyond it was a stream of rushing water that gushed down into an open pipe.

"There it is!" Mario said. "If we swim through the pipe, the water will take us to the Midas River."

"Swim?" Luigi asked nervously.

"It's easy," Mario said. "All we do is —"

"Mario, look!" Toad yelled.

Two Koopa Troopas appeared on the ledge in front of them, blocking their path. They looked like turtles, had red shells, and walked on two legs. They worked for Bowser, and they caused trouble all over the Mushroom Kingdom. They stared Mario and Luigi down, as if daring them to pass.

Mario frowned. "Come on, Luigi," he said. "And a-one, and a-two . . . ,"

Sprong! Mario and Luigi jumped at the same time. They each landed on a Koopa shell.

"One more time!" Mario cried.

Sprong! The brothers jumped again and gave the shells a kick. This sent the Koopas rolling away.

Toad ran up to Mario and Luigi. "You did it!" he said happily.

The Koopas slammed into a wall. Out of

control, they rolled back, crashing into Mario, Luigi, and Toad like they were bowling pins.

"Aaaaaaaaaaah!" the friends cried as the force sent them flying into the rushing water.

The fast-moving stream carried them through the pipe. Bright sunlight greeted their eyes. The water carried them down the stream until the sound of water became a roar.

"Mario, is that what I think it is?" Luigi asked.

"It is," Mario said. "Hang on!"

The stream carried them right to the top of a tall waterfall. They tumbled down the falls. . . .

Splash! Splash! Splash! The three friends landed in Tadpole Pond. Mario stuck his head out of the water and looked around. A friendly face was looking down at him.

"Mario, you are seeking something. Frogfucius knows all."

Mario smiled. Frogfucius was one of the wisest creatures in the Mushroom Kingdom. He looked like a green frog with a long, white beard and a purple crown on his smooth head.

"We're on a quest to save the princess," Mario said, climbing out of the water to stand with Frogfucius on a flat rock. "We're looking for six magic mushrooms. We think one of them may be here."

Luigi and Toad climbed up on the rock, shaking themselves dry. Frogfucius nodded to them.

"Ah, yes, the magic mushroom," Frogfucius said. "The item you seek is in Melody Bay."

"Thanks!" Mario said. Melody Bay, home to the famous composer Toadofski, was just a short trip around the pond.

The friends said good-bye to Frogfucius, then headed for Melody Bay.

"Do you think Toadofski will give us the mushroom?" Luigi asked.

"Toadofski is a good guy," Mario said. "I don't think we will have a problem."

Soon the sound of sweet musical notes drifted to their ears. They turned a corner to see Toadofski, his yellow hair peaking out beneath his mushroom cap, playing a tune on a small flute. He was sitting in front of a glittering green mushroom.

"Toadofski! Good to see you!" Mario cried.

Toadofski stopped playing. "Mario! Luigi! Toad! Have you come to hear my latest composition?"

"Of course, of course," Mario said. "But we need your help, too. Princess Peach has been kidnapped. We need six special mushrooms to rescue her. And you have one of the mushrooms we need."

Toadofski looked alarmed. "My precious green mushroom? But it is my inspiration! I don't know if I can part with it."

"But it's for the princess!" Toad pleaded.

Toadofski took a deep breath. "Perhaps,

perhaps," he muttered. Then he looked at Mario. "I will give you the mushroom — in exchange for a song!"

Mario became nervous. Toadofski already knew all of Mario's best tunes. He would have to think of something new — and quick. It was the only way to save the princess.

"I'll do it!" Mario said. He took the flute from Toadofski and closed his eyes. He took a deep breath. The music that flowed out of him came from somewhere deep inside of him.

Toadofski closed his eyes and listened to the tune. When he opened his eyes, he clapped his hands.

"Magnificent, Mario! What do you call it?" he asked.

"I call it . . . ah . . . *Falling Down a Waterfall*," Mario said.

"I love it!" Toadofski said. "Mario, the mushroom is yours!"

A Maze and a Mushroom

"Thank you, Toadofski," Mario said. He reached down and plucked the glittering green mushroom. Just as with the first mushroom, a wave of light swirled in the air, and a mushroom-shaped clue appeared.

Mario tucked the green mushroom in his pouch. Then he looked at the clue:

F C O B R E E L S E T   S M O A R Z C E
Jump to find the answer.

Mario took off his cap and scratched his head. "*Jump*? Like this?" He bounced up and down. Then he looked down at the clue,

hoping the strange words would make sense somehow. But nothing changed.

Luigi looked at the clue, too. Then his eyes lit up.

"I've got it, Mario! We need to jump over the letters, see? Jump from *F*, to *O*, to *R* . . . ,"

Mario realized his brother was right. If you jumped over every other letter, the words made sense. "Forest Maze," Mario said. "That's where we will find the next mushroom."

Toadofski clapped his hands. "Ah, the Forest Maze!" he said, with a dreamy look in his eyes. "Such an inspiring setting. I once wrote a song there titled 'Lost in a Labyrinth.' I know a shortcut there, if that will help."

"There's no time to waste!" said Toad anxiously. "We must save the princess!"

"Then follow me," Toadofski said.

Toadofski led them around Tadpole Pond to a path that wound through a meadow. Where the meadow ended, a forest began. Toadofski stopped and pointed to a path between two pine trees.

"Follow that path until you come to the Forest Maze," he instructed. "I hope you are able to rescue the princess. That Bowser has no appreciation for good music at all!"

"Thank you for your help," Mario said.

Toadofski bowed with a flourish. "My pleasure, Mario. Thank you for your song!"

As Toadofski turned and headed back to Tadpole Pond, Mario, Luigi, and Toad stared down the new trail. This forest looked friendlier than the dark and gloomy woods where Cybele the Sorceress lived. Mario stepped in first, and Toad and Luigi followed.

As they walked through the trees, Mario found himself whistling the tune he had played for Toadofski.

"What's that up ahead?" Toad asked.

A thick wall of green hedges stretched out in front of them. The wall was broken up by an opening that clearly looked like a doorway.

"It's the Forest Maze," Mario said. "The third mushroom is in there somewhere."

Luigi stopped. "I've heard that you can get lost in there forever," he said. "What if we never come out?"

"We have to try," Mario replied. He stepped inside the maze.

The thick green hedges formed narrow passageways.

"Let's stick together," Mario said. "I've already got to look for four more mushrooms. I don't want to have to look for you, too!"

"Which way should we go?" Toad asked.

Mario shrugged. "We've got to start somewhere." He turned to the right.

Luigi and Toad followed closely behind as Mario led them through the maze. They turned left. Then right. Then left. Then right again. Then left. . . .

"Aaaaaah!" Toad cried.

The three friends had turned right into a sleeping yellow bug. It had a long body like a caterpillar's, brown spots, shoes on its many feet, and a single flower growing out of its head. It appeared to be sleeping.

"That's a Wiggler," Mario said quietly. "Don't wake it up. It'll get really mad."

They tiptoed past the Wiggler, then made another right turn. Then a left turn. They turned and turned, and walked and walked. But there was no sign of the mushroom — or a way out of the maze.

Finally, they came to a spot in the maze where they could choose one of many directions to travel.

"Which way do we go now?" Luigi asked.

Mario turned around in a circle. "I don't know," he replied. "Maybe we do eenie, meanie, minie —"

"Wait!" Toad cried.

Mario stopped. "Another Wiggler?"

"No," Toad said. "Your pouch. It's glowing!"

Mario looked down at the pouch slung over his shoulder. Glittering light sparkled through the fabric. It lit up the entrance to the path on his left.

"I think the mushrooms are telling us something," Luigi said.

"You might be right," Mario said. "Let's go this way!"

They hurried down the path, and around the corner they found a sparkling orange mushroom!

"Perfect!" Mario cried. He plucked the mushroom, and another clue appeared.

RYS'OTE LISE
This clue is like eggs.

"*Eggs*? The clue is in a shell?" Mario wondered out loud.

"Maybe the clue is fried or boiled," Luigi guessed.

Mario smiled. "Or scrambled! Scrambled eggs, just like Mama used to make! The clue is scrambled!"

"You're right!" Toad said, his voice high with excitement. "If you unscramble the letters, the clue says YO'STER ISLE!"

"What do you know?!" Mario exclaimed.

"Maybe Yoshi can help us find the next mushroom."

"First, we have to get out of here," Luigi pointed out.

Mario tucked the brown mushroom in the pouch with the others, and they continued down the path. They didn't have to go far before they saw an exit.

"We did it!" Toad cried.

"Ouch!" Luigi yelled.

"Ouch?" Mario wondered.

He looked up. Two brick pillars rose up on either side of the exit. On top of each pillar stood a Hammer Brother. They looked like Koopas, but each wore a green helmet on top of its head. They were throwing hammers down on Mario, Luigi, and Toad.

"You can't take anything out of the Forest Maze!" one of the Hammer Brothers shouted.

"Oh yeah? Who made you boss?" Mario shouted back.

"Bowser, that's who!" cried the other

Hammer Brother. He threw down another hammer. *Bonk!* It landed on Mario's head.

"Hey! That hurt!" Mario cried. He jumped as high as he could, but he could not reach the top of the pillar.

"Let me try, Mario," Luigi said. He jumped up higher than Mario, but he couldn't reach the top of the pillar, either.

"Ha! You can't catch us!" the Hammer Brothers jeered.

"We'll see about that!" Mario said. He ran toward one of the pillars, jumped up, and gave the bricks a swift kick. The pillar began to tremble.

"Good idea, Mario!" Luigi said. He began kicking the other pillar.

"Hey, no fair!" one of the Hammer brothers shouted.

More hammers rained down on Mario, Luigi, and Toad. They dodged the hammers, then kicked the pillars. Finally, loose bricks began to tumble down. The Hammer Brothers could not keep their balance.

"*Aaaaaaaaaah!*" They both plummeted from the pillars at the same time, landing outside the exit. Mario raced through the opening.

"That'll teach you to throw hammers at me!" He paused, ready to jump on them, but he didn't have to. Both Hammer Brothers had landed on a sleeping Wiggler. The big bug turned bright red with anger. It glared at the Hammer Brothers . . . and then it pounced.

"*Ow! Ow! Ow!*" cried the Hammer Brothers, as the Wiggler pummeled them with all of its feet.

Mario, Luigi, and Toad ran past. Mario picked up a hammer from the ground and stuck it in his pouch — just in case.

"Thanks, Wiggler!" Mario called back. "We owe you one!"

Yoshi Saves the Day

The friends traveled on until they came to the opening of another large pipe.

"This should get us to Yo'ster Isle," Mario said. "I can't wait to see Yoshi!"

They climbed into the pipe and continued walking. Luckily, the path was clear of trouble — no piranha plants, no Koopas, no Hammer Brothers.

"This is our lucky day," Mario said.

Luigi rubbed his head where a bump had formed, thanks to the Hammer Brothers. "I don't know, Mario," he moaned. "I don't feel so lucky!"

After walking a long way down the pipe, the three hopped out into the sunshine. Brightly colored flowers carpeted the ground, and fruit trees dotted the landscape. Jumping and playing among the trees were several small dinosaurs, each one a different color.

Mario called out to a green dinosaur. "Yoshi! It's me, Mario!"

Yoshi turned and smiled happily. The little dinosaur bounded over to Mario and nuzzled Mario's neck with his round nose.

"Good to see you, too, Yoshi," Mario said. "I missed you."

Yoshi twirled around in a circle, then hopped up and down.

"I can't play right now, Yoshi," Mario said. "I need your help. I have to find a mushroom, one that looks like this." He reached into his pouch and pulled out the glittering brown mushroom.

Yoshi nodded his head excitedly.

"You know where it is?" Mario asked.

Yoshi nodded and jumped up and down.

Mario turned to Luigi and Toad. "If I ride Yoshi, I can get there faster," he said.

"That's okay, Mario," Luigi said. "We'll wait for you here."

Mario hopped on Yoshi's back. The little dinosaur took off at a fast gallop. They rode through the fruit trees, past the other Yoshi, until they came to a tall hill. Yoshi charged up the hill.

The breeze whipped through Mario's mustache as they climbed the hill, and a wave of hope surged through Mario. His dinosaur friend had helped him on so many adventures. Now that Yoshi was with him again, Mario felt like he couldn't fail.

Yoshi reached the top of the hill, where a glittering blue mushroom grew. Mario hopped off of Yoshi's back.

"This is it, Yoshi!" Mario said. He plucked the mushroom. Yoshi's eyes grew wide as the clue appeared out of nowhere.

"Now we find out where to go next," Mario said. But before he could look at the clue, he heard a noise.

Thump! Thump!

"What's that?" Mario wondered.

Spiny eggs rained down from the sky. Mario looked up to see four smiling clouds overhead. Riding in each cloud was a Koopa-like creature wearing glasses.

"Lakitu!" Mario cried. "Not now!"

Around him, the spiny eggs were coming to life, transformed into small, mean-looking turtles with spiked backs. They charged at Mario.

"Yoshi, watch out!" Mario cried. He thought quickly. If he jumped on the turtles, he would just hurt his feet on the spikes. Unless . . .

Mario took the hammer out of his pouch.

Bam! Bam! Bam! He thumped each one of the turtles as it attacked.

But where was Yoshi? Mario turned around

to see Yoshi jumping high in the air at the Lakitu.

Gulp! Yoshi swallowed one of the clouds. With a cry, the Lakitu tumbled to the ground.

Gulp! Gulp! Gulp! Yoshi swallowed the rest of the clouds, sending the other Lakitu sprawling.

"Good work, Yoshi!" Mario said. He jumped on Yoshi's back. "Now let's get out of here before those Lakitu know what hit 'em."

Yoshi bounded back down the hill and through the grove of fruit trees. They found Luigi and Toad playing with some of the other Yoshi.

"Did you get it?" Luigi asked.

Mario nodded. "We were attacked by some Lakitu — but Yoshi took care of them."

Yoshi smiled and licked his lips. Mario removed the clue from his pouch. They all gathered around to read it.

The next clue is mine.

"The next clue is yours?" Mario asked, puzzled.

"No, it's not mine," Luigi said.

"Whose clue is it?" Toad wondered.

Mario sighed. They would never find the next mushroom!

The End?

Yoshi began to hop up and down. When he had everyone's attention, he began to dig into the dirt in front of him.

"What is it, Yoshi?" Mario asked. "Something in the ground?"

Yoshi shook his head.

"Something underground?" Luigi asked.

Yoshi nodded.

"Underground . . . ," Mario said thoughtfully. "I got it! The clue is underground — in a *mine*! It means exactly what it says. Good job, Yoshi."

Yoshi let out a happy yip.

"There are mines right near here, in Moleville," Luigi added.

"Then that's where we'll go," Mario said. "You want to come, too, Yoshi? We could use your help saving Princess Peach."

Yoshi wagged his little dinosaur tail. Mario climbed on his back. "What are we waiting for? Let's find that next mushroom!" he cried.

Luigi and Toad jogged beside Mario and Yoshi as they headed across the island to another pipe. They all climbed in.

The four friends emerged from the pipe onto a rocky plateau. A jagged mountain rose before them.

"Moleville!" Mario cried. "Let's head for the mines."

They walked around the mountain, searching for the entrance to the mine shaft. They quickly located an opening in the mountain — but getting inside wouldn't be easy.

"A Chain Chomp!" Toad cried, hiding behind Luigi. "We'll never get past!"

Chained to a post right by the mine entrance was what looked like a large, black ball. It had two angry eyes and a wide mouth filled with sharp teeth. It snarled and growled, pulling at the chain as though trying to break free.

Yoshi tried to hop forward, but Mario stopped him. "I don't think you can eat *that*, Yoshi!" Mario warned.

Toad turned around. "We'll just have to find some other way in," he said.

"Not so fast," Mario said. He closely studied the Chain Chomp. "I don't think he's such a bad guy. I think he just needs our help."

Luigi shook his head. "Mario, I think you got hit by too many hammers back there. That thing will chomp us right up!"

"Maybe," Mario said. "But maybe not."

Mario slowly made his way toward the Chain Chomp. The creature growled and snapped its teeth.

"Easy, boy," Mario said. "I've come to help you."

The Chain Chomp lunged, and Mario

jumped back. But he didn't jump on top of the Chain Chomp — he landed on top of the pole it was attached to!

"I'll have you out of here in no time," he said.

Thump! Thump! Thump! Mario jumped on top of the pole again and again, pounding it into the ground. The chain slipped off, freeing the Chain Chomp!

"Run!" Toad screamed.

But the Chain Chomp stopped snarling. It smiled at Mario. Then it quickly rolled away.

"See? It just wanted to be free," Mario said.

Toad was still trembling. "Let's find that fifth mushroom," he said. "I don't think I can take any more surprises!"

They entered the mine shaft and found a cart on top of a metal track that led into the mine. Mario and Yoshi jumped in one side of the cart, and Luigi and Toad sat across from them. They grabbed the handle between them and began to pump it up and down.

The cart creaked, then slowly began to

move down the track into the dark mine. Toad began to shiver once again. "I almost forgot about those ghosts," he said. "But now that we're getting closer to having all six mushrooms, it means we're getting closer to seeing those spooky specters!"

Yoshi yipped questioningly and looked at Mario.

"There are ghosts guarding Bowser's Keep," Mario explained. "That's why we're finding these mushrooms. They'll help us defeat the ghosts so we can save the princess."

Yoshi nodded and licked his lips. Mario smiled. "I don't know what ghosts taste like, Yoshi," he said. "Maybe they taste like clouds."

Soon the friends saw a soft glow in the distance. The four sped up until they reached the light. A yellow mushroom glittered in the dark.

"Mushroom number five!" Mario cried. He plucked the mushroom, and the dark mine shaft became filled with light as the next clue

appeared. Mario tucked them both into his pouch as the shaft became dark once again.

Mario pulled a lever on the side of the cart and they pumped the handle again. Now the cart squeaked back toward the mine entrance.

Before long, they were back out in the sunlight. They hopped out of the cart, and Mario took the clue from his pouch.

"Only one more mushroom to go!" Mario said. "Let's see where it is."

2 15 15 19 20 5 18   16 1 19 19

1–26

"Numbers?" Luigi asked. "What are we supposed to do with a bunch of numbers?"

"Maybe the numbers mean something," Toad suggested. "Like one through twenty-six. There are twenty-six letters in the alphabet, right?"

Mario nodded. "That's right!" he cried. He picked up a stick from the ground. Then he drew the alphabet in the dirt. Underneath

the letters, he drew the numbers one through twenty-six.

"Look here," Mario said. "The number two is equal to the letter *B*. The number fifteen is equal to the letter *O*. We just have to turn the numbers into letters to find the clue."

Mario scribbled in the dirt. Then he smiled.

"Booster Pass!" he said. "That's easy. It's right around here."

"Just one more mushroom to go," Luigi remarked.

"You mean one more mushroom to *ghosts*," Toad said gloomily.

Booster Pass was a rocky path connecting the mountain of Moleville to another mountain. The pass crossed a deep ravine. If you got close to the edge, you could see the ground far, far below. The friends hiked a short way up the mountainside until they reached the start of the pass.

"It's so high!" Toad exclaimed.

"Just don't look down," Luigi said reassuringly. "We'll be all right."

Toad took Luigi's advice. As they scrambled along the pass, he kept his eyes on the blue sky above. That's why he was the first to see their attackers.

"Koopa Paratroopas!" Toad yelled. "Duck!"

Mario looked up. The sky was filled with green Koopas with white wings. They descended toward Mario and the others.

"Toad, take cover!" Mario cried. "Luigi, Yoshi, start stomping!"

The winged Koopas bounced all around them like basketballs. As soon as one got close enough, Mario jumped on it.

Stomp! The Paratroopa's wings fell off.

Stomp! Mario jumped again, and the attacker rolled away.

Luigi and Yoshi followed his lead. *Stomp! Stomp! Stomp!* They jumped and jumped until every Paratroopa was eliminated.

Toad crawled out from behind a rock. "Is it over?" he asked.

Mario tried to catch his breath. "It's safe now," he said. "We can —"

Stomp!

One last Paratroopa fell from the sky, thudding into Mario. As he slammed into the ground, the pouch slipped off of his shoulders.

Stomp! The Paratroopa bounced again, this time skidding into the pouch. Mario reached out to grab it, but he was too late. The pouch went flying over the edge off the pass!

"Oh no! The mushrooms!" Mario cried.

Watch Out for Wario!

Mario ran to the edge and looked down at the ravine. He sighed with relief.

The pouch hadn't plunged all the way to the bottom of the ravine. Instead, it had gotten caught on a spindly branch that was growing out of the rock about ten feet below. At least he could still see it — but how could he reach it?

Mario looked back at his friends. "I don't know what to do," he said. "I'm good at jumping *up*, not down."

"I know!" cried Toad. He ran back down the path a little bit, then returned holding a thick vine. "Maybe we can use this to get the pouch."

"Hmmm," Mario said thoughtfully. "It could work. We could lower somebody down so they can grab the pouch."

"But you're too heavy, Mario," Luigi said. "What if we dropped you?"

Mario looked around for something strong enough to anchor the vine to — a tall branch, or a tree stump — but there was nothing around. He frowned.

"You're right, Luigi," he said. "It would work if somebody small was at the end of the rope. Small and light. . . ."

Mario, Luigi, and Yoshi all looked at Toad at the same time. Toad's face turned as pale as his white mushroom cap.

"Oh no!" he said, backing up slowly. "I'm afraid of heights. We Toads like to stay low to the ground."

"But it's for the princess, Toad," Mario pleaded.

Toad shook his head.

"Please, Toad?" Luigi asked. "The princess is counting on us."

Toad sighed. "Okay," he said. "But I'm keeping my eyes closed!"

Mario tied the vine tightly around Toad's little waist. He and Luigi grabbed hold of the other end of the vine. Then they gently pushed Toad over the edge of the ravine.

"Help!" Toad yelled. "There's nothing under my feet!"

"Just a little bit farther, Toad," Mario told him.

Soon Toad was dangling right in front of the pouch.

"Reach out and grab it, Toad!" Mario called.

Toad held out his arms, but with his eyes closed, he couldn't see the pouch.

"Open your eyes, Toad," Mario coaxed. "Just for a second."

Toad slowly opened one eye. "*Aaaaaah!*" he screamed. But he managed to get both hands on the pouch.

"Now lift it off the branch," Mario gently guided him.

Toad freed the pouch from the branch, and Mario and Luigi quickly pulled him back up.

"Good job, Toad!" Mario said. "Now that wasn't so bad, was it?"

"I g-g-g-guess not," Toad said, shivering.

Mario took the pouch from him and slung it over his shoulder. "Now let's go find that last mushroom!"

The four of them continued along Booster Pass, navigating between jagged rocks as they hiked. Soon the end of the pass was in their sights — and so was a shimmering red mushroom!

"That's it!" Mario cried excitedly. He broke into a run.

Then . . . suddenly . . . *THONK!*

Mario's world went dark. Something had fallen onto his head! He struggled to get it off. It felt like a bucket. That could only mean one thing. . . .

"Wario!" Mario cried.

Mario pried the bucket from his head. Above him flew a small yellow plane piloted

by a chubby man. The man had a mustache and wore purple overalls.

"Give it up, Mario!" Wario called down. "Bowser's going to give me a lot of money if I bring you to him. You might as well just surrender."

Mario shook his fist in the air. "Come and get me, Wario! Just try it!"

Wario sneered. He dropped another bucket from the plane. This one landed on Luigi's head!

"Somebody turned out the lights!" Luigi wailed. He walked around in circles, trying to remove the bucket from his head.

"That's all you got? Buckets?" Mario yelled. "Not a problem."

Mario picked up the first bucket and jumped on Yoshi's back. "Come on, Yoshi," Mario said. "Let's teach this guy a lesson!"

Yoshi jumped up, almost reaching the low-flying plane. But the jump wasn't quite high enough. Wario laughed evilly and turned the plane around. He threw down another bucket.

"Dodge it, Yoshi!" Mario called out. The little dinosaur jumped to the side, avoiding the bucket.

"One more time!" Mario cried as he scooped up a bucket and jumped on Yoshi's back. This time Yoshi jumped even higher. Just as Mario planned, Wario flew right at them. Mario waited until the perfect moment, then . . .

THONK! He dropped the bucket right on Wario's head.

"Hey! I'm supposed to do that!" Wario barked. He tried to pry the bucket off of his head, but he couldn't do that and fly the plane at the same time. The plane spiraled out of control and quickly disappeared over the horizon. Wario's voice rang throughout the ravine. "I'll get you, Marioooooooooooooooooo!"

Yoshi landed safely on the pass, and Mario jumped off his back. "That serves him right," Mario said. He walked over to Luigi and pulled the bucket off of his head. His brother looked dizzy and confused.

"Thanks, Mario," Luigi said.

"No problem," Mario said. "Now, let's get that mushroom!"

Mario ran to the red mushroom and plucked it. He put it in the pouch with the others.

Suddenly, a blinding light filled the ravine!

G-g-g-g-ghosts!

"What's happening?" Toad wailed.

"My head is spinning!" Luigi cried.

Mario suddenly felt weightless, as if the light were carrying him somehow. He firmly gripped the pouch.

"Just hang on!" Mario called.

Mario closed his eyes as the light got brighter. There was a strange ringing in his ears. His stomach flip-flopped.

Then, everything stopped. Mario cautiously opened his eyes. Luigi, Toad, and Yoshi all looked dazed, but they were fine. The mushroom pouch was safely tucked under his arm. Whatever had happened, they weren't hurt.

Mario slowly looked around. A rocky fortress rose up in front of them, its stone turrets grazing the clouds.

"What do you know?!" Mario remarked. "We're at Bowser's Keep!"

"The mushrooms must have brought us here," Toad guessed.

Mario began hopping up the castle steps. "Now we can save the princess! Hurry!"

Luigi and Yoshi bounded ahead of them. Even Toad hurried along as fast as his little legs could carry him.

When the four friends reached the castle gate, Toad took a deep breath and looked around nervously. "I guess we should be seeing some g-g-ghosts about now."

Luigi looked worried. "I forgot about those g-g-g-ghosts!"

"Not to worry," Mario said. "We have the six mushrooms, right?" He reached into the pouch and took out the paper with the spell on it. He studied it for a moment. "It's easy," he said. "All I have to do is line up the six mushrooms

in order. Then I say some words and then *poof!* No more ghosts."

Mario started to reach into the pouch to grab the mushrooms. But before he could — w*hoosh!* The pouch flew off of his shoulder!

"Hey! Who did that?" Mario shouted.

An eerie giggle filled the keep. A filmy shadow began to form in the air high in front of Mario's head. As the form filled in, Mario saw two glowing eyes, a wide mouth, a transparent body . . .

"It's a ghost!" Toad yelled. He tried to hide behind Luigi. But Luigi was too busy trying to hide behind Toad. Yoshi just looked at the ghost and licked his lips.

"Give me back that pouch!" Mario cried.

The ghost giggled again, as five more ghosts appeared in the air. The first ghost tossed the pouch right over Mario's head to another ghost.

"Hey, that's mine!" Mario cried. He jumped up to grab the pouch, but the ghost threw it

again, and another ghost caught it. They were too fast for him.

"Yoshi, get them!" Mario yelled. The little dinosaur nodded and jumped up, opening its jaws wide to chomp on a ghost. But the ghost just passed right through Yoshi's body.

The ghosts kept tossing the pouch to one another, laughing as if they were playing some kind of game. Mario frowned. If only he could jump high enough and fast enough . . .

"Luigi! You're faster than me! You try!"

Beads of nervous sweat dripped from Luigi's nose. "But, Mario, they're g-g-g-g-ghosts!"

"You've got to do it, Luigi," Mario said. "Just pretend they're not here. Go for the pouch!"

Luigi nodded. "All right, Mario," he said weakly.

Luigi ran toward the ghosts and jumped for the pouch. His hand swiped against it, but he didn't catch it. As soon as the pouch sailed through the air again, Luigi jumped as high and as fast as he could.

"Got it!" he yelled. He landed on the ground and ran toward Mario, handing off the pouch like a football player. "Do the spell, Mario!"

Mario dove to the ground, covering the pouch with his body. "I need you to distract the ghosts while I set up the mushrooms!"

Luigi looked at the ghosts again, more sweat forming on his nose. But before he could make a move, Toad stepped in front of him.

"If you can be brave, I can be brave, too," Toad said. He turned to the ghosts. "Bet you can't catch me!"

All six ghosts zoomed toward Toad as he zigzagged around the room. One ghost even grabbed Toad and tossed him in the air.

"Helllllp!" he cried, as another ghost grabbed him.

"Just hang on, Toad!" Mario cried. All he had to do was set up the mushrooms. "Let's see. First black. Then green. Then orange. Then blue. Then yellow. And finally, red!"

Mario had the six mushrooms lined up. Now it was time to read the spell.

"Mario! Luigi! Hellllllp!" Toad screamed as another ghost tossed him.

Luigi raced toward Toad as Mario took out the spell and read the words.

*"Eeenie, meanie, minie, mo.
Send the ghosts where Bad Boos go!"*

As Mario read the spell, the mushrooms glowed. A ray of color shot out of each mushroom, forming a shimmering rainbow in the air. Each ray grabbed a flying ghost and wrapped it in colored light.

"Aaaaiiiiiiiieeeeeeee!" shrieked the ghosts. In a flash, they vanished into the lights. Toad tumbled down toward the stone floor, but Luigi caught him just in time.

The rays of light disappeared, and the mushrooms stopped glowing. Mario gave a happy sigh.

"See?" he said. "I told you. No more ghosts."

"Mario! Help!"

Mario's heart began to beat quickly. He knew that voice.

"It's Princess Peach!"

Big Bad Bowser!

Mario charged toward the sound of the princess's voice. He ran through the gate, then into the main hall of the keep.

"Help! Help!"

The sound came from above. Mario raced up the nearest staircase and through the first doorway he saw. He found himself in a round room — the same room as in the sorceress's vision!

"Mario! Please help me!"

Just like in the vision, Princess Peach was trapped in a metal cage that hung from the ceiling. Mario's heart nearly broke when he

saw the poor princess. When he got hold of that Bowser . . .

Mario stopped fuming. He knew had to act fast.

"I'm coming, Princess!" Mario called. Luigi, Yoshi, and Toad ran up beside him. Mario climbed onto Yoshi's back.

"We've got to jump up and get the princess out of that cage," Mario said.

"That's what *you* think!"

A booming voice echoed throughout the room. A big, ugly turtle stomped into the room through a back door. Sharp horns stuck out from his head, and pointy spikes jutted down his back. Metal spikes adorned his collar and wrist cuffs. Equally sharp teeth filled his snarling mouth. His arms and legs were bulging with muscles, and a thick shell protected his back.

"Back off, Bowser, you big bully!" Mario yelled.

"No way," Bowser bellowed. "I've got

Princess Peach. The Mushroom Kingdom is mine. It's time to run things Bowser-style!"

"What style is that? Mean and stupid?" Toad squeaked in a moment of bravery. Bowser glared at him, and Toad quickly ducked behind Luigi.

"You little pipsqueaks can't stop me!" Bowser bragged. "Ghosts, get them!"

But no ghosts appeared. Bowser looked around the room, puzzled.

"That's right," Mario said. "We took care of your ghosts. And now we're going to take care of *you*, too!"

"Oh yeah?" Bowser sneered. He opened his mouth wide — and a red, flaming fireball zoomed toward Mario!

"*Aaaah!*" Mario cried. He quickly jumped to the side.

"I've got more where that came from," Bowser growled. He spewed out another fireball.

This time, the burning fireball bounced

toward Luigi. He dodged out of the way, but the fireball grazed the back of his overalls.

"Ouch!" Luigi screamed. He sat down on the stone floor and rolled around, putting out the flames.

Bowser chuckled. "You're in for a hot time, boys!"

Whoosh! Whoosh! Whoosh! Bowser let loose with a barrage of fireballs. Mario, Luigi, Toad, and Yoshi ran around the room, trying to dodge them.

Slam! Slam! Slam! Slam! In the chaos, the four friends bumped into one another, then collapsed in a heap in the corner. When they got to their feet, Bowser faced them with an evil gleam in his eye. They were trapped!

"Yum, yum!" Bowser said. "Looks like it's time for a barbecue."

"Mario, what are we gonna do?" Luigi wailed.

"It's hopeless!" Toad added.

Hopeless.

The word triggered something in Mario's

mind. The sorceress had said, "Open this — but only if there is no hope left." Mario couldn't imagine a better time to open the envelope she had given him.

He quickly pulled it from his pouch. Inside was a piece of paper with a message written on it:

Once the spell is good and done,
Throw the mushrooms one by one.
What they do I cannot say,
But be sure they'll save the day!

"Sounds good to me," Mario said. He grabbed the black mushroom from the pack. As Bowser readied to launch another fireball attack, he threw the mushroom in front of him.

Poof! The mushroom exploded in a cloud of black smoke. Bowser coughed and choked as the smoke enveloped his face.

"Who turned the lights out?" Bowser wailed.

"Run!" Mario whispered urgently to his

friends. Luigi, Yoshi, and Toad all ran in different directions. Now Bowser couldn't trap them all again.

The smoke cleared. Bowser stomped toward Mario. "Hey! That was a dirty trick!"

Mario quickly threw out the green mushroom. It transformed into a green bouncing ball.

Bop! The ball bounced up and hit Bowser on the forehead.

"Hey!" Bowser yelled.

Bop! It bounced back and knocked into Bowser's snout.

"Stop that!" Bowser complained. He swatted at the ball.

Bop! It bounced into Bowser's belly, but this time he caught it. He hurled the ball right at Mario.

Thinking quickly, Mario threw the pouch to Luigi. Luigi caught the pouch, and Mario caught the green ball before it slammed into him.

"Luigi, throw another mushroom!" Mario yelled.

Luigi threw the orange mushroom at Bowser. With a pop, it transformed into five small hammers that pummeled Bowser's body.

"That's no fair!" Bowser growled. "Give me that bag!" He lunged for Luigi, who hurled the bag at Toad. Toad caught it and took out the blue mushroom.

Before Toad could throw the mushroom, Bowser swirled around and spewed a fireball at Toad. Toad hopped back and threw the blue mushroom out in front of him.

Whoosh! The mushroom turned into a wave of blue water. It doused the fireball, then splashed over Bowser, drenching him.

"That's enough!" Bowser yelled. He angrily charged toward Toad.

Mario quickly hopped on Yoshi's back. Yoshi bounded across the room in one leap. Mario grabbed the pouch from Toad and then jumped away.

"It's not enough until *I* say so!" Mario called out. He threw the yellow mushroom at Bowser's feet. It turned into a puddle of slippery yellow slime.

"*Ah-ah-aaaaah!*" Bowser slipped in the slime, slamming into the floor. He waved his arms and legs wildly, trying to get up.

Mario jumped off of Yoshi's back. He threw the last mushroom, the red one, at Bowser.

"You better leave the princess alone!" he yelled.

The red mushroom transformed into a huge fireball. The flaming ball slammed into Bowser with amazing force. It sent the bully skidding across the floor on the back of his shell. The force sent him flying right out the window!

Luigi and Toad ran toward Mario and Yoshi.

"We did it!" Toad cried.

"Now we just have to save the princess," Mario said. "Yoshi, you know what to do."

Yoshi nodded, and Mario climbed onto his

back. Yoshi hopped underneath the cage that held Princess Peach.

"Jump!" Mario commanded.

Yoshi jumped straight up in the air. As they passed the cage door, Mario reached out and opened it. Then they landed on the ground.

Yoshi jumped again. This time, Mario jumped off of his back and landed inside the cage. Princess Peach smiled and hugged him.

"Mario, thank you!" she cried.

"It's nothing," Mario said, blushing. "Now when Yoshi gets here, you jump on his back, okay?"

The princess nodded. Yoshi jumped straight up again, and Princess Peach hopped on his back. Yoshi landed safely on the floor. Princess Peach climbed down, and Toad and Luigi happily greeted her.

"Last jump, Yoshi!" Mario called down.

Yoshi nodded and jumped one last time. Mario hopped on his back, and the two landed safely on the ground.

"You all saved me!" Princess Peach gushed. "Thank you so much!"

Mario, Luigi, and Toad all shuffled their feet and muttered in reply. There was something about the princess that made everyone shy.

"We got the mushrooms. We took care of the ghosts. We got rid of Bowser, and we saved the princess," Toad said. "Can we g-g-g-go now?"

"Of course," Mario said. Then something caught his eye. "But I've got to do one thing first."

On a table against the wall, Mario spotted a book. He walked over to it and looked at the title. It was *The Book of Spells*.

"I don't think Bowser will need this anymore!" Mario smiled and put the book in his pouch.

And somewhere, deep in a mysterious forest, the sorceress smiled back.